The
Bookworm

by Jon Coley

Prologue

Matthew had a good visit with his brother, Chadwick. He seemed to be more lucid, more attached to reality this morning. That was good. Rare, but good. It was almost like being with the big brother he looked up to in his childhood. The one who read him a bedtime story almost every night when he was little. On his good days, one would wonder why the man had been committed at all. But Matthew knew it was all too temporary. An orca could swim comfortably in a pool that was filled with the tears he'd shed over his brother. Their parents were both gone now. Chadwick's hair had some gray on the ends now, and it had been this way for so many years now. Soon enough the poor fellow would begin his maniacal rantings about other worldly creatures and dark phantoms. It was such a shame, heart breaking really.

At least today was a good day. The weather was pleasant, and so was the visit. Chadwick had been painting again, the brushstrokes huge with vibrant colors. One could feel the mountains and valleys just by looking at the canvas. Matthew left his big brother at the home for the mentally disturbed and climbed into his old red truck. Slowly the crankshaft turned until the engine finally sputtered to life. It was a long drive back his house. His back was going to be angry about it too. At least the fall weather was cooperating, and the scenery pleasant this time of year. He wanted to get there before his son got home from school.

Young Brian was such a bright kid. He and his wife were quite proud of him. Matthew was amazed at how driven the boy could be. What a self starter that child was. The only real fear they had was that he was such a bookworm, which was something that made him so much like his uncle.

Chapter 1

Brian loved crisp, autumn mornings. The air was cool, but the sun was quite warm. Light breezes gently tickled the hairs on his arms. He took a deep breath and began his morning trek to school. As the front door closed, he heard his mom telling him to have a good day in her high, almost sing song morning voice. He waved back at the window instead of yelling. That was his nature. He hated having to talk. It was so ... exasperating.

What he did love, though, was reading. The truth was that he loved reading more than playing, which was quite rare for a fifth grader, or any kid for that matter. With the morning home rituals completed, Brian was ready to start his short journey to his favorite place, the private school that he had earned the right to attend for free through an academic scholarship. The school was located in his community, but he was one of the few kids from his working class neighborhood that attended.

It was a good morning to walk to school. The nearby park still proposed the same problem for him that it did every day, though. In the middle of the park, there was a stream. It was bigger than most, but not quite big enough to be called a creek. The water moved fast enough to be heard, the proverbial babbling brook. Brian knew it would be a great deal easier to use the footbridge, which gave easy passage at a wider, but picturesque, point of the stream. This, of course, was one of the main attractions of the park. But he, once again, skirted that path and followed the stream to a more narrow crossing point. There, next to the woods, he crossed with a leap, the cold water splashing off his well worn shoes. Every morning was the same in this way. He would shirk his self prescribed duties to face his fear, as irrational as it was, only to admonish himself for taking the longer route. One day, he would have to cross that old bridge. He didn't want to end up like his Uncle Chadwick, afraid of his own shadow. Plus, he thought he heard a big animal rustling around in the nearby woods.

The journey between Brian's home and his beloved school wasn't too far. He did, like always, have to rush after crossing the stream. Getting to school on time was his responsibility and he took it seriously. So he broke into a jog. Soon the woods gave way to a clearing, and the noble spire of the institution's main edifice appeared, like an arrow aimed at the sky. He set foot on the concrete sidewalk just as the tardy bell began to ring. Once again, he made it just in the nick of time. Sure he would have preferred to get to campus early, if only to spend more time in that marvelous library filled with old and new books of all kinds and genres, but he was glad to have avoided being late for class. It had been a long week at home during fall break. All his old reading materials had been voraciously consumed long ago. He was eager to get back to his studies.

After retrieving his literature book from his locker, Brian made his way to his first class. His shoes squeaked as he walked due to the stream water and the morning dew, but his weren't the only ones making that noise. Unlike everyone else, he had already read more than half of the books related to the excerpts in his textbook, another of his self prescribed goals. Part of it was competition, though he knew he was the only one who took the the time to actually do this. But he thoroughly relished the stories, especially the classics. He loved fantasy, historical fiction, folk tales, or any good literature really. Reading was his super power, and in his mind, the only advantage he truly had in this world.

Most of the other kids were already seated. This didn't bother him here like it would have in his old school, where everyone always seemed to stare at the last kid walking in for some reason and there were always the ubiquitous thumps on the ear if you weren't paying attention. The neighborhood kids were more rough-and-tumble. The he classes here were only about half the size of any given public school. The "Dormies," as they were called on campus were mostly foreign students. About half of them were Asian. Most of the rest were a mix of European nationalities with just a few Africans scattered throughout the grade levels. They were all pretty studious, so chatter was kept to a minimum. Brian was a "Day Dog." These were usually students from well-to-do, local families. He wasn't well-to-do, though. He was a scholarship kid. Most of those were for athletics, though there were no dumb jocks on campus to be sure. He was the only academic scholarship recipient in his grade level. There were a few others like him in the high school, but he was the only one in lower school. Still, he was much more comfortable in these hallowed halls than anywhere else, really. Plus, he'd earned his place.

Like the other kids in his literature class, Brian began to get set up. His teacher still hadn't arrived, but this wasn't too unusual either. Students were trusted to behave well on campus, unlike the daily situation in his former public school. If you couldn't cut the mustard here in any way, you were simply dismissed. He respected this policy, as draconian it may have been, because it was enforced fairly, no matter how rich or powerful one's family was. There was due process too, with probation, but immoral misbehavior was not tolerated. This actually made Brian even more comfortable. Here he knew where he stood. He hadn't sported the first black eye since he enrolled, which was a definite check in the win column to his mind.

A few minutes later, the general noise level fell to a complete hush. A man strolled through the door with his nose in an old book. He walked behind the desk and set the book down, still reading it while standing. Some of the other kids looked at each other. Finally, he put a bookmark between the pages and slowly closed the book. Brian noticed a faint cloud of yellowish dust. The old book must have been dug out from deep in the library. Mrs. Griffin, the librarian, was usually incredibly meticulous about keeping her books in pristine shape.

"Good morning. As you can see, I am not Mrs. Courtney, unless she's a particularly ugly woman."

He grinned and a few kids chuckled.

"My name is Mr. Dyer, and I have a message from Mrs. Courtney to her students. First, she regrets to inform you that she will not be returning to her teaching duties until after spring break. She had to return to her hometown to take care of some family business. She wished to convey that she still had high expectations from each and every one of you and that she fully anticipated you all being on schedule when she returned."

Mr. Dyer was slightly odd to Brian. He wasn't what one would expect to see in a substitute teacher for a private school. Sure, he was well dressed. But it was his demeanor, even his build that was askew. He wasn't a skinny old bed of wrinkles with thin wisps of white hair floating about his crown. Nor was he a corpulent pile of flesh belonging to a man believing that his body's sole purpose was but to carry his head around. No, Mr. Dyer was different. While not particularly tall or overwhelmingly muscular, he was lean and well built, what his mom would have called big boned. (She didn't mean it the way most people do.) But he also wasn't like his physical education teacher, who only focused on his body and was continually dreaming up new ways to torture little nerds like him. He was so in-between. All that with what seemed to be a dry sense of humor and general good nature was ... off putting to Brian. He didn't know what to think about the man. It didn't matter really, he supposed, because he was obviously stuck with him for the next few months until his favorite teacher returned. It was going to be a long, cold winter.

Chapter 2

The school day was reasonably uneventful. Classes moved on without too much drudgery. Brian was still as glad as ever to be in those hallowed halls. Every moment was validation of his ability and tenacity. He worked hard to be there and enjoyed it thoroughly. Even his physical education class was okay to him. Some days were harder than others in gym class, but there was far less harassment from the other kids in comparison to his old school, which was nice. Sure, Coach Mathis was tough on him, but he was like that with everyone. Brian didn't take it personally, and sometimes he even had fun.

It wasn't until recess that Brian saw Mr. Dyer again. He was on his way to the library to return some of the books he'd read over the break, and to hopefully retrieve a book that was on hold for him that covered the psychology of phobias. The librarian, a nice enough lady, seemed nonplussed when he requested it. This didn't surprise him in the least. It wasn't the usual book for a fifth grader. But he needed to know why people had such strange fears, and he didn't want to end up like his Uncle Chadwick. As he opened the door, he saw Mr. Dyer with a his nose in a book. The man looked up and gave him a nod.

"It's a beautiful outside, Brian. Surprised you're not playing with the other kids."

Brian didn't know what to say. He nodded back to his new teacher and walked up to the librarian to drop off his books. He love the feel and smell of the wax finish on the wooden shelf. He leaned on it as the librarian checked the status of the book in her computer. Unfortunately, it still wasn't in.

"Sorry Brian," said Mrs. Griffin, "High school kids never turn in their books on time, even around here."

"Thank you anyway. I'll check again tomorrow."

Mrs. Griffin nodded and resumed her work. For the first time in weeks, at least at school, Brian didn't have a book in his hands. It felt so strange to him. He thought about browsing, but for some reason, he felt the need to get out of there. However, he had to pass by Mr. Dyer on the way to the exit. Much to his chagrin, the man looked up from his book as he passed by.

"Didn't have your book, huh? Well, may as well go out and get some sunshine. There won't be many more days like today this year. Consider it a blessing. Psychology books can be so dull, except for Jung. His stuff is pretty cool."

"Yes sir," Brian answered awkwardly. He passed by the man and exited the library. For the first time, he actually went to the school playground of his own accord. This was the one area that was just like his old school. At least it felt that way to him. Some of the kids were running laps, working off their demerits. Most of them were paying tag or swinging. He wasn't interested in any of that, so he decided to take a walk, the one physical activity he enjoyed because it cleared his mind. It wasn't until a few minutes later, with the brisk walk illuminated his thinking, that it occurred to him. Mr. Dyer knew his name even though he didn't take attendance this morning. And he knew what Brian wanted to read!

*

Later that afternoon, it was a perfect day for a walk through the park. Brian knew that it was the way he should go, but he found himself standing between the woods and the other path leading to the bridge. Perplexed by his sense of duty in battle with his sense of dread, the decision couldn't be made. It was when he remembered his encounter with his strange new teacher that he at last decided to walk by the woods and jump the stream at its narrower point again, regardless of the cold damp that would inevitably sink into his toes. Usually a sense of guilt and shame would ensue, but today he was too concerned with the strange happenings at school, so those emotions ebbed. The image of his new teacher surrounded by golden dust haunted him.

Instead of focusing on what he couldn't control, Brian used his alone time during the walk to consider his fear of the bridge. He wasn't afraid of bridges themselves. He had traveled innumerable bridges with his family on various trips. It was only that one bridge in particular. Why did his heart race every time he tried to set foot on those old, rough wooden boards? Even if it were a rickety safety hazard, which it wasn't, he was a fine swimmer. It was one of his few athletic skills, other than walking. The bridge occupied his mind for the entire walk home.

"Good afternoon, Sweetheart!" his mother sang out cheerily as he entered the kitchen. He just waved and smiled at her. "Your father should be home soon. He went to visit your Uncle Chadwick. How was school today?"

"Fine. We got a new Literature Teacher today. He'll be replacing Mrs. Courtney until after Spring Break."

"Oh. I hope everything is okay," his mother said with a trace of concern as she pulled dinner from the oven. Brian shrugged.

"I don't know. The new teacher's name is Mr. Dyer."

"Hmm, Dyer. I'm not familiar with that name. Well, I'm sure everything will be just fine. Do you have a new book to read?"

"No," Brian said flatly, but decided to add, "The book I wanted's not in yet, so I went out to recess."

His mother smiled in surprise, "Wonderful! Nothing wrong with reading, but you should always make time to play with your friends."

He nodded, uncommitted to the idea, and left the kitchen. That was the longest conversation they'd had in weeks. It was exhausting for him, but he was glad he could say something to make her smile. She had the kind of smile that began in the heart, came up, and illuminated everything around her. At least something positive could be gained from this strange day. He had no idea how strange his days were going to get.

Chapter 3

The next day, Brian decided to avoid the bridge again. This was a little different than his usual routine in that he made the decision as soon as he got out of bed instead of doing so on the way to school. There was no sense in lying to himself. He was a little off kilter and saw no need to prolong the discomfort. That fear would have to be faced sooner or later. This much he knew, but things just weren't going his way lately. The proverbial deck was stacked against him for now.

He made it to school a little earlier than usual, but not early enough to stop by the library before his first class. He would go during recess again, although he had to admit to himself that the weather, with the crisp air and warm sun, would be missed. This rarity reminded him of his new teacher and the previous afternoon's meeting. He shook the thought from his mind and let it fall away. What were the odds of his new teacher being there two days in a row?

Whatever those odds were, Brian soon found it to be the case. As he walked by the stained glass windows in the hallway, taking a moment to enjoy the warm sunlight, Brian sensed it. Somehow he knew Mr. Dyer would be there with his nose in a book, golden dust motes flittering about. It didn't matter how he felt about it, really. He was going to go in regardless, but it just made things ... uncomfortable.

As he opened the ornate wooden door and smell the fresh scent of wax polish, his intuition was confirmed. Mr, Dyer was seated at a table with his nose deep in a book, just like the day before, just as Brain suspected. His eyes traveled to the librarian's desk. Mrs. Griffin wasn't there. Of course no other kids would be there this time of day either. They were playing outside, enjoying the sunshine. It was just him and his odd new teacher. Brian's skin, just barely, began to crawl.

"Brian! Just the person I wanted to see," Mr. Dyer said with a grin. He got up from his seat and walked over in that off putting way. It wasn't aggressive, but it wouldn't be ignored. Brian noticed that he carried an old book with him, and just a little bit of golden dust danced around it.

"I'm afraid that your incredibly boring psychology book isn't in yet. I was asked to relay the message if you came in. Mrs. Griffin had a meeting. But listen, I've got this book for you. You seem like the kind of kid who can appreciate good literature."

Mr. Dyer handed the obviously old tome to him. Brian instinctively took it and opened to peruse the pages. In spite of himself, he was incredibly curious. The book was large, with super thin leaflets for pages, like a Bible. To his astonishment, he saw that the text wasn't printed, but written in script. How old was it?

"It's a first edition, you know. Anyway, if you promise to take care of it, I'd like you to borrow it for a while. Let me know what you think about it. It's not an assignment, by the way."

Brian looked up from the script, "Yes sir. It would be an honor. I've never seen a book this old, I mean, rare."

Mr. Dyer laughed, "The older things get, the rarer they become. I can totally relate to that."

Brian laughed, in spite of himself once again.

"Also Brian," Mr. Dyer said, "I'd go out and enjoy the weather again before you dive into this. Like I said, there won't be many more days like this."

"Yes sir," Brian stammered, "And thank you very much."

Brian did go out for recess. It was difficult not to go sit down in the library right away. He knew Mr. Dyer was right, though. The seasons were changing fast. So before venturing out of doors for the second day in a row, he secured the book in his locker. Again, he felt it was best to walk around the playground area, not being one for tag or sitting on swings. To his surprise, Ceara, a Dormy, walked up beside him. She was in some of his morning classes, Mr. Dyer's class included. She was an American girl, which was a little rare for the Dormies, with brown hair and green eyes. He knew her about as well as he knew anyone at the school. That is to say, they had spoken with each other once or twice.

"Mind if I join you? It looks like good exercise," she said.

Much to his surprise, Brian answered without thinking, "Sure, why not. I'm trying all kinds of new things lately."

*

The walk home was taken by the woods, once again. He decided to avoid the bridge right after his last class. Though he was in a hurry, there was no need to fool himself. If he went to the bridge, he would waste valuable time deliberating over the decision and backtracking, because he knew in his heart that he wasn't ready yet. The footbridge would have to wait. Brian took the longer route between his school and his house, and got his feet a little wet by jumping the stream. Along the way, it occurred to him that he crossed between two different worlds twice a day. His upscale private school, where most of his classmates were from rich families, was quite different from his lower middle class neighborhood. This didn't really bother him much, because he was proud of his parents and the life they provided for him. On the other hand, there was certainly nothing wrong with having money. Most of his classmates were pretty nice to him too. Besides, where else would he get his hands on such treasures like the old book he carried in his bag right now? He couldn't wait to sit down at his writing desk. It was hand built by his dad with care. It could literally be feel when rubbing your hands across the smoothly sanded wood grain, the love, care, and craftsmanship. There, in his own holy of holies, he would discover the mysteries it had to offer.

If he had only known, he would have waited.

Chapter 4

"Good afternoon, Darling," his mom said, "How was your day?"

She was chopping vegetables for a salad. There was a pleasant smell coming from the oven and steam was rising from the stovetop. Brian noticed that she was still wearing her smock from work.

As usual, a million thoughts rushed through Brian's head. They pushed and shoved, bumped and bruised one another until one of his usual answers was produced.

"Fine thanks."

He was glad she nodded and accepted his reply with a smile. Sometimes the awkwardness was too much to take. He loved his parents dearly, but it was so hard to communicate with them. It wasn't their fault at all. Speaking was such a tiresome thing for him, and he loathed small talk. Not hearing it, necessarily, but participating in it. The sad thing was that it was even harder for him to converse with those he loved the most. It wasn't a lack of things to talk about that stopped him. It was that too many thoughts pushed their way from his brain all at once. They bottlenecked in a traffic jam in his mind and only select habitual phrases seemed to be able to slip from his tongue. He always thought that he would be able to handle the words better when his brain got bigger, but there were so many more words to handle. His vocabulary grew exponentially, which was both a blessing and a curse.

"We're having dinner a little early today. Your father just got home from visiting his brother. Would you mind setting the table, Dear? We're eating in the kitchen this evening."

"How is he? Uncle Chadwick?"

"Um, fine right now. He's been having a good couple of weeks, according to your father."

"Good. I'm glad."

"Yes, Yes. Things are good for now. When you're finished, call Your dad in too. Everything's just about ready."

Their dinner was delicious. Brian chided himself for not telling his mother how good the kitchen smelled when he walked in. Another thought that got lost in the traffic jam. His parents chatted with each other in between bites. This, in its own way was a comfort to him. They really seemed to enjoy each other's company. He'd seen many other parents who seemed to resent each other. It occurred to him that it was no way to live. Of course, there were plenty of kids in his old school who's folks were divorced. The style of separation was totally different at his current private school. Kids spent so much time away from their families there, especially the Dormies. Plus, there were all the different cultures and nationalities. The world seemed to get so much bigger ever since he changed educational institutions. Great, more big words. Why couldn't he just say schools in that mind of his?

Brian was glad of his situation, though his father was emotionally strained caring for his mentally ill brother. All the same, Brian knew he was lucky to have parents as good as his.

"So how was your day, Son?"

Brian swallowed his food as he realized that his parents were both looking at him waiting for a reply. His father had asked the question.

"Fine thanks."

"That's all I got out of him when he walked in," his mom chuckled.

Some words, just a few of the hundreds in his head, miraculously squeezed through the bottleneck. For a change, Brian didn't waste the opportunity.

"Well, I got a new book today. My new teacher gave it to me."

"Oh, is that so, son?"

"Yes sir. It's very old, written in script. I've been waiting on another book from the the library, which isn't in yet, so he gave it to me."

Brian reached behind his chair into his backpack and pulled out the the old tome. He held it up for his parents to see.

"That is one big book, son. I haven't seen an old book like that since I was a kid. My brother used to read them, you know."

"Now Dear, I'm glad you're so involved in your studies, " his mom interrupted, obviously not wanting the conversation to turn to his uncle, "But I hope you're getting plenty of fresh air and sunshine too."

"Well, yesterday and today I did. Basically I just walked around the playground with my friend, Ceara."

"A girl?"

It was his fathers turn to save the conversation, "Now dear, let's not interrogate him. I'm willing to bet you're wanting to dive into that book." Brian nodded. He wasn't too embarrassed, red cheeks aside, but he definitely did not know what else he say. This conversation was well beyond his usual limit.

"That's just fine, son. I'm glad you're making friends. Keep reading your dictionary sized books and keep being sociable. You'll do great. Trust me."

Brian nodded again, put his book away, and resumed eating dinner, grateful to have the distractive activity. He was relieved when his parents began discussing other things between themselves like the latest gossip at his mom's job and the local news. The pressure was off.

Finally it was almost bedtime. His curiosity had been eating at him all afternoon. Brian went about his usual routine with quickness and efficiency. with zeal, he made ready to fish the book from his backpack. Being a bibliophile at heart, the first crack of a book was a kind of a ritual for him. He loved the smell of the print, the feel of the pages between his fingertips. This book's odor was different, of course. Its great age saw to that. That was no deterrent to Brian's pleasure, though. So under the low lamplight on his writing desk, he began to read, one finger caressing the page under each word and the fingers of the other had resting on the smooth finished wood of his writing desk.

It was an epic poem written in script with decorative flourishes aplenty. Such works usually had monsters and wars. Obviously, this tome would be no different. The key was to glean the underlying meanings and to excavate nuggets of truth. Brian was ready to do exactly that.

Chapter 5

"Here we go again," Brian said to himself as he stared at the footbridge. It just sat there, staring back at him blankly as the water passed by underneath. The scene was actually beautiful in its own way. Birds were singing nearby. The stream babbled softly. Why did it seem so ominous to him? The need to post danger signs all around was hard to fight, as absurd as that would be. He had to see it this morning for some reason that he couldn't quite understand. A little thought, no, an emotional pull niggling in the back of his mind. He knew he wasn't going to cross it, but he just had to be there. It had to be faced. He had to let it know that he saw it. There wasn't enough time to tarry, so he turned on his heels and took the longer route again, trekking toward the woods.

It truly bothered him. He wasn't the kind of person to do things based on fear. In his heart he was a fighter, though an unlikely one. A short, skinny boy that seemed too shy to even play on a playground with other kids, that's what he was. But he wasn't shy at all. In fact, he liked his peers, even at his old school. It's just that there was so much in the way. Now he had a new challenge in his heart. Sure the bridge had been there all his life. He had crossed it before, long ago, relatively speaking. But now it called to him, provoked him, dared him to cross. He knew intuitively that if he couldn't face this new challenge, he may fall down that slippery slope and end up just like his crazy uncle.

But he would face the bridge another day. Today he still needed to get to school. His mind wandered as he skirted the edge of the woods, the damp autumn leaves brushing against his pants. He had read the old, mysterious book well into the night. The seeds of adventure had been planted in the first few pages. Questions brewed and simmered in his mind. There were monsters and creatures, both great and small. His brain hadn't yet had time to digest it all. There weren't those little bubbles of truth popping up yet, which is what he truly loved. All this was running through his head. He was nearly running, trying to get himself to school. That's probably why he tripped over the dragon's tail.

He was quite lucky. The great beast took no notice of him at all. To the dragon, Brian was just another little animal scampering around as it made its way through the forest. Sure, if it got hungry enough, Brian would make a tasty treat. But it had other things on its mind. This new forest would make a fantastic nest! Treasure could be looted and hoarded. Its great scales shimmered in the dappled patches of sunlight as the beast-that-shouldn't-be went about making its instinctual plans.

For his part, Brian scrambled back to his feet. His brain was processing the current impossibly before him as best it could, which wasn't really all that good. His heart was doing its job, pounding in his chest. Inner heat, outer cold, and hyper focus all set in at once. He didn't know whether to fly or fight. He did neither. Instead, the young boy, no bigger than a teacup chihuahua in comparison to this massive dragon, went into the woods, into the lair of the beast.

The monster went about sniffing here and there, gazing at the trees. It's wings, leathery and bat like in appearance, were tucked behind its humongous shoulders, running about three quarters the length of its back. There were little horns (comparatively speaking) running along its spine. They appeared to grow ever more sparse in transition from haunches to tail. A faint, golden dust seemed to dance all about the creature's body. Brian thought his brain was playing tricks on him as far as that was concerned, he still didn't trust his eyes. The dragon walked on all fours, snaking its long body through the woods, rubbing and scratching through the trees. Its scales randomly knocked swathes of bark clean off of several full grown trunks.

The neck was long and serpentine. It's overall physique was slender, but obviously powerful and sinuous. This was a beast meant for flight. It wasn't until it flicked its tail, felling two trees in the process, that Brian perceived how heavy and powerful the thing truly was. He felt like a grasshopper looking at a great trout, just realizing the wet terrain it was standing on was only the water's surface, and that was all that kept him from becoming a dinner. The hairs on the back of his neck stood straight up. He had to do something. But what? That question was never answered because just as he seemed to be sensing the dragon's presence, it sensed him.

Instinctively, Brian jumped behind a tree. Just as instinctively, the dragon pulled itself up to face him, like a great rattlesnake readying to strike. It's wings unfurled, taking up all the scenery around them. They could have been described as magnificent with their dark, translucent membranes allowing hued spectrums of color through from the blazing morning sun. The unmistakable golden dust flurried about them too, but to Brian they were terrible to behold. The beast opened its wide maul, displaying rows of sharp, ferocious teeth. Then it did something peculiar. It chomped down on one side of its jaw, making a clicking sound. A tiny spark lit the inside of its mouth. Then it belched, but clamped its lips down to hold it in. This would have registered as comical, if it weren't for what happened next. The creature made a face like it was about to whistle a tune. Instead of a melody, a hideous stream of fire shot out from its face arching directly onto the tree that he had been using as a shield.

Brian sprang from behind the blazing branches and shoulder rolled across the ground behind another thicket. As he once again scrambled to his feet, a strange new emotion welled up in his heart

- anger. Sure, he was frightened out of his mind, and completely confused by the absurdity of the situation, but this abomination before him made him ... just plain mad. It was one thing to wander around a place and accidentally knock a few trees down. But being destructive on purpose and setting things ablaze like it owned the place, not to mention all the small animals whose lives were destroyed without out even a second thought, that was unacceptable. The dragon had to go. It didn't belong here! It hadn't earned the right to be here. Brian's very bones began to vibrate with the sentiment. It was this anger, fury even, that compelled him to do one of the stupidest things in his entire life.

"Hey, you overgrown maggot! Get outta here."

Yes, it was a stupid thing to yell at a dragon, but at least he threw a rock at it too. He struck it on the snout, which probably was barely noticeable to the beast, but it did grow really agitated. A

41

tumultuous growl projected from its face, and it sprang into action.

Brian got a lot smarter really quick. A charging dragon has that effect on a person. He ran like he never had before, weaving in and out of the trees. The dragon followed suit, snapping at his heals. It was amazing that such a huge beast was so agile, so fast. He had no time to wonder about that, though. The harder he ran, the more vicious the dragon became, snarling and biting at him. He could feel its hot breath huffing on the back of his legs. Its long body carved a path along the ground between thickets and over rocks. Smaller trees that couldn't bend snapped like twigs and fell. Mounds of soil and stones popped up from the earth and showered back onto the ground as the mythical monster plowed its slapdash path. It was one of those stones that finally put an end to the chase.

One fist sized rock ricocheted off the whirling dervish and landed right under Brian's foot, causing him to misstep and stumble. The dragon froze instantly, inertia ignored, impossible as that should have been. Brian could feel the heat of its rancid breath falling on top of him. The odor would have disgusted him if he weren't so busy watching his life flash before his eyes. He turned over onto his back to face it, surely the last face he would ever see. Slowly and deliberately, the dragon lowered it's massive head, peering at him with one eye, a black abyss in itself. There was a look of recognition and triumph on the creatures face. It pulled its head back, clicked its jaw, belched, and engulfed Brian in flames.

Mercifully for him, everything went black.

Chapter 6

Brian screamed. All the other kids in the classroom jumped.

"It looks like someone didn't get enough sleep last night," Mr. Dyer said wryly.

All the students laughed, except Ceara, who looked back at him with concern. He was sitting at his usual spot, the desk in his first period class. How did he get there? One second, a dragon was roasting him alive, the next he was making a fool of himself at school. What happened? Could it have all been a dream? Some kind of hallucination? It seemed so real.

"Okay, folks. Settle down. Please turn to page three hundred twenty-six. There are some questions there for us to look at together."

As he opened his textbook, Brian thought to
himself that the questions he had wouldn't be
found on any page in any textbook.

Between classes, he went to the restroom and
took an inventory. He wasn't burned or scratched
as far as he could tell. His clothes weren't torn or
even singed. His shoes had a little dirt on them,
but that was no different than usual, given his
daily travels. There was no sign of his previous
struggle with the dragon, which was both good
and bad. It's never good to fight a dragon, most
would readily agree. But Brian knew what he saw.
He also knew that it was just plain crazy. His
Uncle Chadwick was just plain crazy too.

When recess time came, Brian was sure to get
some fresh air. The weather was still good, though
not as crisp as it was in the beginning of the
week. The light breeze still felt good on his skin,
though. He walked the perimeter of the
playground. It was beginning to become a habit.

This, he hoped, would clear his head. As he passed the swings, Ceara caught up with him.

"You feeling okay today?"

"Not going to lie, I've been better."

"I knew something was up when I got to class this morning. You were the first one there and you were dead asleep in your desk. I was going to nudge you, but Mr. Dyer came in right after me and told me it would be best to leave you alone. He said you'd probably need your rest. I guess you told him you were sick or something?"

Brian ran his hand through his hair.

"No, I didn't. Truth is, I don't even remember getting to school this morning."

Brian stopped mid sentence. How did he get to school? Why did Mr. Dyer want to let him sleep?

Was the dragon still in the woods? He shook his head as he walked.

"Well, you seem better now. I guess you just needed some fresh air."

Brian nodded, "And good company too."

Ceara grinned. The two young friends continued there walk around the campus playground until recess was over. After that, they went their separate ways to attend afternoon classes. Brian meant what he said too. The fresh air and good company really made him feel better, even though he might have to face a dragon on the way home.

*

There was no dragon in the woods, just trees and autumn leaves gently dancing in the breeze. Like his earlier inventory, that was both a good and bad thing. It's never good to run into a giant, flesh eating, fire belching monster all alone in the middle of a forest. But it's also never good to hallucinate crazy things that aren't there either. Brian looked around cautiously. There was no trace of the beast. There should have been ruts in the ground and broken trees everywhere. None of those things were to be seen. He was just about to give up his search when he saw a thin trace of smoke trailing up above the tree line. Small ribbons and wisps floated up and dissipated into the afternoon air.

Deeper into the woods he traveled. There it was. One lonely stump, charred and still smoking. The flames were gone, and there was no danger of a wildfire, but there it was just the same. Brian was so relieved. He had some proof, at least for himself, that what he'd experienced that morning was real. He gingerly placed his hand on the stump. It was still warm too. Sure, there were more questions than answers. But for now, Brian was glad that his sanity seemed to remain intact.

He didn't want to chance running into the dragon again, so Brian navigated his way out of the woods as quickly as possible. When he got back to his usual route, he walked double time. His mom would be worried if he got home too late. But for now, he was content to let his thoughts drift. There were far too many things in his head to contemplate, to ponder. Unfortunately, they would have to wait.

Chapter 7

"Did you get plenty of exercise and sunshine today, Dear?"

Brian looked up from his plate. He had been lost in thought again. So many questions stirred in his brain that it was hard to focus.

"Yes, Ceara and I walked the perimeter of the playground. It was a beautiful day today."

"Ceara?" his dad asked, "Is that the same young lady you were walking with yesterday?"

Brian nodded. He didn't know what else to say.

"Our little boy is growing so fast," his mother exclaimed.

"Yes, absolutely. So how was your day, Dear?"

Mercifully, his parents turned in conversation to one another again. Brian was able to finish his dinner and, once again, get lost in his thoughts. Does Mr. Dyer have anything to do with all this? Wasn't there a dragon in the first story of that ancient book? Did the old book have anything to do with what happened? Brian began to think he just may be losing his mind after all.

Later that night, Brian got ready for bed. His brain was still racing. Unable to sleep, he tossed and turned. It was too hot under the covers, then too cold with them pulled down. After an hour of not being able to sleep, he sat up and looked over toward his writing desk. Earlier, he had decided to forego reading the book for the night, but it seemed like it was calling to him. In the soft shadows, it appeared innocuous enough, but he just couldn't shake that feeling, a slow, continuous pull in his gut. Exasperated, he finally decided to get out of bed. Not wanting to wake his parents, he tiptoed over to the desk.

After his eyes adjusted to the light from the reading lamp, he opened the old book again. The slow reading due to the old script actually relaxed his mind. There were stories within stories. No mention of dragons, but other monsters certainly took part in the action. These were basically undead army battalions. Most kids would have had nightmares after reading such things, or watching a movie with these creatures in it, but Brian felt calm and sleepy. He finished a section describing a tragic battle over some long forgotten enchanted land, then he yawned. Finally, he marked his place and closed the book with care. It was way past time for bed. Once again, he tiptoed across his bedroom. This time he slept.

Chapter 8

The next day started out a little better. For a moment, Brian even considered walking toward the bridge, but he decided to forego that battle for a little while longer. He left home in plenty of time to take the route by the woods, jumping the stream and barely getting his feet wet. Even so, he was sure to give the edge of the trees a wide berth. But there was no trace of the dragon, which was a pretty good thing.

Each morning had become just a little cooler. Brian noticed the pattern. Winter was on its way. This just provided him with all the more impetus to walk faster. He actually made it to school a little early. There wasn't enough time to visit the library, but he did take his time before going to class and was able to get all his books and supplies in order.

The first period class went well. He enjoyed his studies, and was pleased to see that the impromptu nap he had taken the previous morning didn't put him too far behind. Mr. Dyer, Ceara, and all the other students seemed to have completely forgotten about his outburst too. That was one of the other benefits of private education. The students were always ready to get back to business as usual. He would've been hearing about it for weeks at his old school. The kids here, though, had too much to do to bother with trivial things like one of their peers screaming in class.

Ceara joined Brian for their daily recess walk. He was grateful that she didn't bring up what had occurred. She seemed happy to enjoy the day with her friend. He wasn't sure why she preferred walking with him, though he recognized that she wasn't as silly as some of the other girls were when left to their own devices. He really did appreciate her company. And while he couldn't stand small talk, conversation was easier with her than with anybody else. He was also glad that she didn't bring up the previous day's episode again. She seemed more than content to enjoy the autumn afternoon with her friend. Perhaps it was because she missed her family. He wasn't sure, but he had no idea how to bring it up either.

The walk home was blissfully uneventful. There wasn't a hint of unusual sound coming from the woods, no crackles or growls, no smell of smoke or displaced dust. The weather had warmed considerably in the afternoon, but was still quite pleasant. The breeze was nice too.

Brian had decided to leave the dragon where it belonged, in the past. Perhaps when he was older he would investigate the matter further. After all, one can't have random dragon encounters plaguing his neighbors. That just wouldn't do at all. He even decided that he would take another look at the footbridge over the weekend when he had some free time, maybe just take a few steps, feel the wood creaking under his feet. Just a step or two to feel things out, that would do the trick. He was feeling pretty good about himself as he fished his key from his pocket to unlock the front door of his home. Of course, all that changed when the huge green hand grabbed him up and snatched him inside.

Instantly, Brian became weightless. There is a logical explanation for everything. The sudden loss of gravity he was experiencing was simply due to the fact that he was flying through the air into his living room, perfectly logical. Luckily for him, he landed on the couch as gravity reasserted its dominion. Unluckily for him, he found himself staring up at a gigantic ogre.

The monster was at least eight feet tall. This was plainly evident because it was hunched over to fit inside the house, yet the nape of its neck brushed against the ceiling. It seemed to be in a total rage. Greenish brown muscles were quivering all over its wide torso. Though it had a protruding gut, it was still manifestly powerful looking. The stench given off was overwhelming too. Back and forth it paced in the tiny space (for an ogre, anyway), becoming more agitated by the second, grumbling and snarling. Mini earthquakes vibrated with every step it took. Brian was afraid to move. He could feel the entire house shaking.

After it threw him onto the couch, it seemed to be more concerned with its new surroundings. The brain of young Brian raced, trying to formulate an escape plan, but the creature was between him and the door. He could run further into the house, but he'd never make out the back door in time.

Golden dust, Brian noticed but barely registered, floated around the creature as it paced back and forth. Then it turn to the mantle above the fireplace where the family portrait had been lovingly placed by his mother years ago. The monster paused, peering at it closely. It was a portrait of the four of them, Brian, his parents, and his Uncle Chadwick. He was a good bit younger then, but it was the only picture of the entire family they had. The ogre sniffed it, then its eyes shifted over to Brian, disdain oozing from its visage. The creature roared furiously, its arms stretched out, spanning the entire living room. It balled up both fists, but only used one to smash the portrait and the mantle into smithereens.

Strangely, once again, Brian's terror converted instantly into pure anger. It was a special kind of anger, indignation. This rancid buffoon had intruded into his home. It had no right to be there, destroying his family's precious possessions and property. He wouldn't allow it! That was why he did something really stupid yet again.

"Hey! You nasty green idiot! Get out of my house!"

The ogre paused, confused. Then the rage came back tenfold. It lunged for him. Brian's stupidity dissipated quickly, which was a very good thing, because he had to jump off of the couch just before the ogre's anvil like fist came down, breaking the furniture piece into two distinct, but completely disheveled halves. Splinters and dust, golden and otherwise, flew everywhere.

Brian sprinted toward the back door. The monster was surprisingly fast, though. Plus it had an incredible reach with those huge, apish arms. Just as he was pulling it open, a filthy green hand reached out from behind and above him, slamming the door shut. Brian ducked instinctively and dove between its feet. It was a narrow escape, but he managed to get to the other side of the monster, which did not make the thing happy in the least.

Another massive fist came down as Brian jumped away. It left a hole in the floor that looked like a mouth gaping in terror. Brian escaped just over the threshold into his bedroom when he, once again, became weightless. This time he wasn't flying, only floating. The ogre had finally caught him and seized him by his collar. Slowly it turned him until they were face to face. It's wide hooked nose sniffed him. Golden dusted entered and exited its cavernous nostrils. The creature smiled menacingly and licked one of its thick tusks that was protruding from its lower lip. It was relishing the victory.

Slowly it raised its free hand and closed its fist. The ogre's countenance changed. Suddenly, it had the face of pure delight. Brian fully understood that this wasn't good. The beast was thoroughly pleased that it was finally going to crush him like a helpless cockroach, crunch and splat. Over and down the fist came. Everything, mercifully, went black.

Chapter 9

"Brian, dinner's ready!"

Brian sat up with a start. He reached up and grabbed his head, his face. It was all still there. He had a pounding headache, but his brains weren't splattered all over the floor. They should have been. Another check in the win column for sure. How long had he been asleep? Slowly he climbed off his bed. He looked into the hall. The hole in the floor was gone, like it was never there, like nothing happened.

"Brian?" his mom called again.

"On my way," he called back.

He stepped onto the hallway floor where the hole had been, testing it for support. It was fine, no sign of any damage. Brian shook his aching head and wandered into the kitchen where he was greeted by his parents. They were waiting for him at the dinner table.

"Hey there, sleepy head," his dad jibed.

"Hi, sorry I didn't help set the table."

"No worries, sweetie," said his mom, "I think you needed your rest."

Brian nodded and sat down to join them.

"You'd better take it easy with that old book of yours, son," his dad commented, "That's probably why you're so tired."

"I think you're right."

"Are you still getting plenty of exercise and sunshine?" his mom queried.

"Every day this week, actually."

"I can tell. You've gotten a lot more color. It's doing you good."

"Thanks," he said to his mom as he reached for his fork.

"You're right, Dear. He is looking a lot better nowadays. Not that you looked bad before. Listen son. Keep it up, okay? And do take it easy with all that hard reading. I know you enjoy it, and that's great, but I don't want you to end up shut in your room all day. There's a big world out there. I used to tell my brother that when he had his nose stuck in a book."

His dad trailed off. He didn't mean to steer the conversation toward his uncle. Brian knew this, but he was woefully unequipped to ease the tension in the room.

"Did I tell you about what my manager did at work today?" his mom interjected.

His dad took the cue, obviously relieved.

"No, Dear. How was work today?"

As his parents turned the conversation to their small talk, Brian ate his dinner slowly. He was still preoccupied with the ogre, the dragon, the book, all of it. But he knew his dad was right. Whatever ever was happening to him was too much. He needed to take it easy. His throbbing head agreed.

After dinner, Brian went to the living room. There was one thing that was still bothering him. The monster had destroyed the family picture. He had to see it. Much to his relief, it sat on the mantle, unharmed. He examined it closely. The image was fully intact. But then he noticed it. Up in the corner, above his Uncle Chadwick's head, there was a tiny crack in the glass. He put his finger on it. It wasn't there before, he knew that for a fact.

He felt a tingle and a tiny pinch on the end of his fingertip. When he withdrew his hand, the crack was gone. Brian's eyes widened. A tiny speck of golden dust flittered up and disappeared.

"You alright, dear?" his mom asked.

When did she walk in? How long had he been staring at the picture?

"I'm fine, Mom."

"Good. I know it's stressful thinking about your uncle. And I know you're worried because you two have so much in common. But sweetie, you're not him. You are you're own person. Always have been. Ever forget that."

"I know. It's just been a long day. A long week, actually."

"Well, it's almost time to get ready for bed. Get some sleep, okay?"

"I will. Good night."

Brian went about his usual bedtime routine, his mind spinning all the while. But he was true to his word. The book called to him again. He refused to answer, as tempted as he was. It took a couple of hours. He was restless and his head still hurt a little, though eating his dinner had helped. The darkness, at long last, overtook him. He was too tired to dream.

Chapter 10

The next morning, it looked like it might rain. Brian was sure to put an umbrella in his backpack. The air was pleasant on his walk to school. It made him feel refreshed. He needed that. After his two battles with other worldly monsters, he needed a real win too. Too bad he didn't get it.

As he trudged toward school, deep in thought, his feet did a terrible thing to him. They wandered toward the footbridge. It wasn't until he saw the first wooden plank that he froze. Why had he come this way? He wasn't even thinking about the footbridge, though it was always lurking in the back of his thoughts. Now here he was, staring down at the old wooden structure. His childhood fears, relatively speaking, began crawling up from the depths of his mind. His heart began to race. Something always told him to stay away from this place. He knew must never come here alone. Until recently, those conditions were acceptable. It was easy enough to do. But now, he just couldn't live with it. Brian put his foot down.

If he were able to see all the ramifications, he would never have taken that step - ancient white and black holes converging with worm holes jumping between, ripples in the spacetime continuum, and quantum particles rearranging probabilities. He couldn't see all that. No one could. He could see, however, the explosion of golden dust. For a moment, he was disoriented. The golden cloud blotted out the morning sun. Brian waved his hands in front of his face, trying to clear the dust away. That was when the troll attacked.

Claws, teeth and dirt snapped and grabbed at him. Instinctively, Brian jumped backwards, tumbled and rolled to the ground. When he scrambled to his feet, it was all gone. There was no dust, no troll, just an old footbridge with a pleasant stream passing by underneath. Not being one to require second bidding, he ran as fast as he could in the other direction away from the footbridge, taking the route by the woods to school. He ran the whole way, clearing the stream in one leap with room to spare.

The rain was a blessing. No one noticed how tired or sweaty Brian was when he got to school. He took a moment to dry off as best he could in the restroom, which helped. Getting the sweat out of his hair and off his face made him feel a little better. He caught his breath and walked into class. Though he wasn't late, he was considerably later than his usual habit, which meant that both Mr. Dyer and Ceara gave him concerned looks as he walked to his desk.

"Got caught in the rain?" Ceara asked.

"Um, yeah. It snuck up on me. I have an umbrella, but...."

"Okay class, let's get started," Mr. Dyer announced.

The class was by no means noisy, especially compared to where Brian used to go to school, but there was still some shuffling about and paper rustling to do as the students got settled in. As Mr. Dyer continued with his lecture, Brian noticed that his teacher seemed distracted. He kept looking in his direction too. Did he know what happened this morning? How could he? He shook the thought from his still damp head.

At recess, Ceara walked with him again. It didn't take her long to break the silence.

"You seem distracted today."

"More than usual?"

"A little, got something on your mind?"

Brian continued walking for a moment before answering.

"Let me ask you something. Let's say you were given a gift from someone, but it was ... defective."

"That happens. There's nothing wrong with returning it, you know?"

Brian shook his head.

"What if that gift was dangerous, and maybe the person gave it to you like that on purpose?"

"Is this person Greek?"

"I don't think so, why?"

Ceara shrugged.

"There's a saying. Beware of Greeks bearing gifts. Either way, sounds like a big jerk to me."

Brian laughed, paused, and realized that he hadn't laughed all week. He stopped walking and began cackling. Laughter is contagious, so Ceara joined in. After a moment, they resumed their path around the playground.

"That was a little bit crazy," Ceara said, though she seemed to appreciate the levity.

Brian grinned and replied, "You have no idea."

After recess was over, the two friends went their separate ways. They each had their own classes to attend. But Brian made his decision and he had Ceara to thank for it. She had helped him clear his head. The weekend was coming, and he was going to pay Mr. Dyer a visit. Like his friend said, there's nothing wrong with returning a defective gift.

Chapter 11

It was the weekend, a beautiful Saturday morning. The rain had brought in cooler weather, but still mild enough. Brian and his parents sat down together for brunch. They usually only ate two meals on Saturday, preferring to sleep in a little bit later on their day off, or at least half day off, so a late breakfast and early lunch was usually combined into a nice midday feast. It was a weekly family tradition that he loved, because they all worked together to prepare the meal. The familial cooperation and camaraderie was more than a comfort to him. It was like a glue, in his mind, that kept his family together and whole.

"I'll be going to work a for a half day today, so supper will be a little late."

"That's fine, Dear. I need to go visit my brother today. It's best to go while things are good. There won't be many more days like this. Will you be all right on your own for a while, Son?"

Brian looked up from his waffle and nodded. His father's words ringing in his ears.

"Actually, I was thinking about returning Mr. Dyer's book to him today. He lives over on Heard Street, according to Ceara."

"Ah, well that's fine. If he's not home, just leave it in his mailbox."

"But don't stay out too late, Dear. I want you home before supper time," his mother said.

Again, Brian nodded. His mother put her sandwich, which was a work of art in its own right, down and said, "Everything is changing. We all have our own agendas. I'm going this way, you're going that way, and even our little one has his own plans."

Brian's dad broke the reverie.

"Now, now, let's not get too nostalgic. There'll be plenty more weekend brunches for us to have together."

Brian's hands shook from nervousness. He wasn't so sure, but he did hope so.

*

The walk would have been quite pleasant if Brian weren't so preoccupied. It was finally jacket weather, so he sported his favorite hoodie. The old garment was a little too big for him last year, but he'd grown just enough for it to fit perfectly. From time to time he would switch the large, old book from one hand to another, but this was more out of habit than necessity. Heard Street was a little longer distance away in another direction from his usual routes to school, but it didn't take too long to

75

walk. Soon he arrived at Mr. Dyer's residence. It was a nice house, and certainly didn't seem to be the domicile of a malevolent magical mastermind. He closed his eyes to summon courage and to erase the accidental alliteration from his head.

Mr. Dyer's mailbox was the small metal type that hung on the outer wall under the roof of a little , covered front porch. Brian thought it was a nice looking home, not much different from his, really. There was no way the book would fit in that tiny mailbox, though. He would never leave such a book outside in the elements either, even under a porch roof. That wasn't his actual plan anyway. It was only a mental crutch to keep himself from chickening out. This was the moment of truth. After taking a deep breath and gathering his courage, he rang the doorbell.

"Just a moment," a lady's voice called from inside the house.

Did he have the right place? He'd gotten his information from Ceara, but she could have been wrong. He was about to turn away and step off the porch when the door popped open.

"Hi there, you must be Brian!"

The lady had a bright, broad grin on her face. She seemed to be about his mom's age, which made sense.

"Yes, ma'am. Is this the Dyer residence?"

"Don't be silly. Of course it is. I'm Mrs. Dyer. Mr. Dyer told me that he was expecting you. He's finishing up some work in the library. Please, come in."

It must be said that it is generally a bad idea for a child to go into stranger's house. Specifically, it wasn't a good idea for Brian either, but he was getting desperate and something had to change.

He only hoped he wasn't jumping out of the frying pan and into the fire. It was only just after he crossed the threshold that the thought registered in his mind. Mr. Dyer was expecting him!

"Would you like some tea, Dear?"

He didn't want any tea.

"Yes, ma'am, that would be very nice."

Her face lit up, which was an impressive feat, given that she had already been grinning ear to ear.

"Wonderful! I've been working on a new recipe. My husband is too set in his ways to try anything new, so we'll try it together. You sit here and I'll be right back."

Brian obliged. He didn't have much choice in the matter. Mrs. Dyer disappeared from the living room into what he could only assume was the kitchen. There was some muffled clanking, then she reappeared carrying a tray with a silver teapot, a small canister, and two teacups with saucers and spoons. A fresh bouquet of scents seemed to follow her, spicy but sweet. She sat down on the chair across from him, placed the tray on the coffee table, and began working.

After making the hot tea concoction for both of them, they each gingerly took a sip. Brian wasn't a tea person. His family were coffee drinkers through and through. Even if he didn't like it, he knew he'd grow to be one too. It was an integral part of his persona. But this tea was wonderful.

"How is it?" she asked expectantly.

"It's absolutely delicious, which I didn't expect."

Brian stopped. The wrong words made it through the bottleneck yet again.

"I mean, It's unexpectedly delicious."

This seemed to satisfy her greatly. She clasped her hands together in front her and rested them in her lap.

"Why, thank you Brian. I was thinking that it was too much chai."

Brian wasn't sure what chai was. All he knew was that in went in tea sometimes.

"Well, I'm not sure. It's like art. People talk about it like it sets their heart on fire. I don't know about that. All I know is what I like, and I really like this."

"Good afternoon, Brian," said Mr. Dyer.

In one motion, Brian put the cup down and stood up, clutching the book.

"I'll have you know that this charming young man thinks my tea is a work of art," said Mrs. Dyer.

"I don't disagree, Honey. But sometimes I feel more like your canvas than your patron."

Mrs. Dyer chuckled, "Well, I'm just going to sit here and enjoy my magnum opus while you two go talk."

"Fair enough. Brian, shall we go to the library?"

"Yes, sir," he nodded.

Mr. Dyer led him out of the living room and into the small library. He walked around the desk, piled with various old books, and sat down in his well worn office chair. The room looked like it was cut out from any given university library, like a nook was magically separated and transported to this house. Brian immediately loved it. Two walls were completely covered with book shelves, floor to ceiling, which in turn were overflowing with books of all sizes, colors, and conditions. In spite of himself, he felt a level of comfort only a true bibliophile could understand.

"Please, have a seat," Mr. Dyer said as he pointed to the other chair, "Feel free to leave the door open if you like. My wife never listens to a word I say anyway."

The joke was meant to make him feel more at ease, but Brian sat down, still clutching his book.

"I suppose you're here about all the monsters," he said rather nonchalantly. The words punched him in the gut.

"The ogres and dragons, just like the ones in this," Brian said holding up the old book.

"Yes, just like in the book. I'm sorry about the ogre showing up in your house, by the way. I truly believed it would attack you from the woods, like the dragon."

Brian's head was spinning. Could this be real? He instinctively knew it was dangerous to confront the man, of course. However, he was just beginning to realize how hazardous the situation actually was. At least he was close to the door, which he did leave slightly ajar. But he had a feeling it really didn't matter. He was the proverbial fly caught in the spider's web.

"Why would you do this? You gave me some sort of ... cursed object?"

"Actually, I did nothing of the sort. That book is just that, a book. It isn't cursed or magical.

There are two magical, for lack of a better word, things in this room. I'm one of them, and I'm talking to the other one."

"What? What are you talking about? I'm a fifth grade kid, just like any other."

"Oh no, you're not like any other. You're just like me, a bookworm."

Chapter 12

Upon realizing that he'd stood up in anger, Brian stopped and sat back down. This was madness. What was this man saying? And yet, there was something to it. An instinct, deep down in his being, had just sparked.

"What do you mean? Yes, I love to read. I'm a bookworm. That's just an expression."

"Yes and no. A bookworm is a person who loves to read. True, but we are the real bookworms. Our kind, the ones who were originally called that, were the lovers of the written word. But we studied the authors' work to learn more about our enemies."

"You mean Monsters?"

"Yes, mostly, but there are other enemies as well. Monsters are crude and violent, but the sentients, they are far rarer, and far more dangerous. The book I gave you has no sentients in it, so you wouldn't appear on their radar, as it were. I wanted monsters on your mind, so they would be more likely to sense you first. Let me explain things another way. Are you familiar with Taoism?"

Brian nodded, "Vaguely. It's the Yin and Yan, isn't it."

"Yes, but before I continue, I'm not a Taoist. In fact, my wife and I attend church just a few blocks away. This is just the best way to demonstrate our situation."

Mr. Dyer stood up to continue speaking. He drew the famous Yin and Yan symbol with his finger in the air. To Brian's amazement, golden dust followed the trail. He was literarily drawing the Taoist circle in midair.

"As you probably know, the Yin and Yan are two serpents, sometimes thought to be dragons, actually. One represents order. The other is chaos. The eyes are the opposite. There is some chaos in the side of order and even some order hidden in the heart of chaos. This is all well and good for eastern philosophy, but what most people don't know is that chaos is always trying to get in."

"You mean that the monsters don't belong here, but they want to take over?"

"That's right. You see, words have power. That's why there are ancient tales of magicians chanting spells. Long ago, when chaos and order weren't in balance, it was the written and spoken words that sealed the deal, so to speak. This is why there are so many writers who say that stories just come to them. Writers tell the stories, but these are actually spells reinforcing the walls, the ABZU."

"What is that?"

"Oh, an ancient Samaritan term relating to the abyss, the sea, the realm of chaos. That's where we come in, the bookworms. This spell, weaved so long ago, banished magic into the chaotic realm along with all its inhabitants. Unfortunately, the situation is dynamic, unstable. THEY always want in and will go to any lengths to do so. We are the last vestiges of magical people on this side. We can sense the ABZU, the border between order and chaos."

As he spoke, the picture of the Taoist circle began spinning in the middle of the room. The dust glowed golden in the late afternoon light. Sometimes the Yin swelled larger in size, sometimes the Yan reciprocated. It was an uneasy balance.

"It is our calling to banish the monsters when they try to come in. We are the only ones who can sense them while still between worlds."

Brian sat silent for a moment. It made sense to him, all of it. He knew it to be true. But it was crazy! How was he supposed to accept it?

"Mr. Dyer, while the story is compelling, don't you think it's odd that you're drawing with magical golden dust in midair?"

"What? Oh, yes. It's ... firmament."

He waved his hand through the magical illustration, scattering the dust back into the ether.

"Most people can't even see it, just bookworms and some writers. Most authors aren't magical at all, just like most avid readers are just that, literature fans. In fact, the Council doesn't worry much about writers nowadays. They naturally fall into their place, keeping the spell reinforced without even knowing. But bookworms, we're a different kettle of fish. We have to find each other, carve out a territory, protect one another from the sentients, and the madness."

One thought pervaded Brian's mind, Uncle Chadwick.

"I'm sorry that I had to be so cloak-and-dagger with you. It was imperative that you come to me. Part of the spell, from what I understand. It's important that bookworms find each other before maturity. That's when the sentients can more easily sense us, whether we know about them or not. There hasn't been a bookworm in this territory for decades, really. That's why the Council sent me. This home is on the outer edges of my territory, but it overlaps with yours. I'm here to help you fight the monsters for a while, and to ready your mind for the evil ones."

"So it was you who got rid of the dragon and the ogre?"

"Yes, and I was impressed that those were your first monsters. Mine were ghouls. They're just as evil, but not so ... cantankerous."

"Wait. If the monsters can sense us, and we can sense them, why should we even go near the ABZU?"

"Like I said before, they always want in. They are looking for us. If they can get past us, they can enter our world in full strength without being anchored to their point of entry in the ABZU. No one would stand a chance. We are the only defenders against them. Besides, they can still cause trouble for the unsuspecting bystanders. The proverbial woman walking down the street who is killed by a falling piano. Sometimes that's fate, but sometimes it's the chaotic realm intruding. Chaos wants to destroy, to kill. That's what it does. It's why houses are haunted. It's why nations break down into civil war. Genocides erupt between otherwise good and moral people for reasons that make absolutely no sense in retrospect. But we have the chance to snuff it out at the root. Tell me, Brian, have you ever sensed the evil of a place?"

Brian nodded. His heart was pounding in his chest. A vision of the footbridge crossed his brain. Mr. Dyer smiled, knowing he made his point.

"Don't worry, kid. You're much stronger than you know."

He wasn't so sure about that.

Chapter 13

The two sat in silence for a few moments. Brian digested the information as best he could. He was a bookworm. He had a job to do. Was this why he always took on so many responsibilities? Was it in his blood? Did he come from an ancient line of defenders?

"Listen, Brian. It's important to know that you don't have to slay the dragons. In the ABZU, you are just as strong as the monsters. They have anchored themselves to a small part of this world, but every opened door can be closed again. Let the firmament lead you. It's how you can sense them ahead of time, and how you can find the door."

Another moment of silence passed.

"I have one more question, Mr. Dyer."

"Absolutely. The more you know, the better."

"How did you get to me so fast? I mean, with the dragon I was getting roasted. The ogre was about to crush my skull."

"Ah, I forget how unreal this seems to the uninitiated. In the ABZU, time and space is irrelevant. You might say it's relational to the action at hand. As soon as I sensed disruption in the firmament, I stepped in. You weren't hurt with either creature, really. The rebalancing of the firmament has disorienting effects. That's why you were unconscious. There are skills that I will help you to develop for combatting this. It gets easier over time too. Like I said, most people can't see it at all. We can. It's our ... gift."

Brian laughed, "Some gift!"

Mr. Dyer cracked a smile too.

The sun was getting low in the sky as Brian and the Dyers stepped onto the porch.

"It was lovely to meet you, Brian," Mrs. Dyer said.

"You too," said Brian, "Thank you for the tea."

Mrs. Dyer's smile broadened, another feat.

As he traveled back home, the afternoon's conversation turned over and over again in his mind. He switched the book from hand to hand every so often. Mr. Dyer insisted that he keep it, because it would be useful. Brian had no intention of reading it for a good while, but he knew that his mentor was right. As he traveled home, hoping to be in time for dinner, he kept an eye out for firmament. His gift was still developing, but he knew he could already use it for self defense. Thankfully, there was none to be found, for now.

When he made it home, his mother noticed that he still had the book and asked him about it.

"He wanted me to keep it. It's a gift."

"Well, that's very nice of him, Dear," said his mother as she finished preparing dinner while he was busy setting the table.

Brian went into the living room, where he saw his father looking at the family portrait on the mantle.

"How's Uncle Chadwick?"

"Hmmm? Oh, he's doing quite well, Son. It's been a good couple of months for him. The voices have been quieter. I know it's only a matter of time, but it was a good visit. He was almost his old self again."

Brian nodded, "Dinner's ready, Dad."

"Well, what are doing standing around here for? Let's eat. I've starved."

Brian grinned as the two of them joined his mother in the kitchen. The food was delicious. He enjoyed listening to their small talk, even though he didn't have the mental energy to join in. There was so much to think about. But at least he had some answers. And for the first time in his life, he was hatching a real battle plan in his fertile young mind.

Chapter 14

It was a clear, cold Sunday morning. Brian's favorite hoodie did its job, though. He adjusted the hood back a little on his head so he could see better. The bridge still had a little frost on it, gleaming in the sunlight, but not enough to make anyone lose their footing. He squinted his eyes and concentrated. There it was! He could just barely make out a small area of golden dust flittering about at the far end of the bridge. Even if people could see it, like him, most would have missed it. He had for years, but never again.

Years. The anger welled up inside him, the indignation. How many kids had been tripped up while crossing the bridge? Had anyone been injured or worse? The evil of the place was repugnant. But this was his territory. That thing was not welcome here. He stepped onto the footbridge and into the ABZU. Firmament exploded into the morning. With it filling his vision, Brian could see into the past. All the scrapes and bruises the creature had caused little children to endure out of pure spite. A young man in a canoe with a concussion, not being able to steer away from the bottom of the bridge. True little pieces of chaos. All this happened in an instant, the very one in which he made eye contact with the monster.

The troll was on the far side of the bridge, biting a fish's head off. A grotesque creature it was too, dressed in rags and covered in filth. It's nose was equal in size to the rest of its head and its mouth looked like someone threw a bunch of misshapen stones into it from a distance for teeth. The fish guts and decay didn't help either.

"There you are. I hope you enjoyed that fish. It's your last meal here!"

The troll looked over to him and grinned, "BBB-RRRRR-III-AN."

So it knew his name. Fine! That was all that it was going to have to take back to his world. Brian charged.

*

The troll faced him and began galloping on all fours, it's overly long arms reaching across several planks at a time. It roared, teeth grinding and filthy talons flashing. Several boards cracked under its weight. Golden dust, firmament, gushed out everywhere. The bridge was almost completely ensconced. The troll was ready to tear that annoying little boy to scrumptious little pieces, for he was the one who held the key to this world. Closer. Closer. He would taste delicious. The little fool wasn't running away this time. Ready to jump, go for the kill!

*

Brian ducked. He knew from the heavy vibrations shaking his knees that the creature had little control of its own momentum. Sure, it was ferocious and dangerous, but it was no dragon. Just as it's broad belly passed over his head, he sprang upward, using the troll's own inertia against it.

*

Up the troll flew, farther than it wanted. The boy looked up at it. The monster scratched at his outstretched arms, just out of reach. It could feel the old world pulling. Up, up, up. Then golden dust closed around it. The stupid boy disappeared. Then, just as it feared for years, it fell into the darkness. Accursed home.

*

"Brian! Are you all right?"

He looked up. After the troll was sucked through the door, so much firmament went up with it. The vertigo was sickening. He fell to his knees, panting, fighting the blackness.

"Brian, Brian!"

"I'm okay," he said as he pulled himself to his feet using the wooden rails of the footbridge to keep steady.

Mr. Dyer grabbed him by the elbow.

"I tell you you're a bookworm and the next day you're slaying dragons."

Brian shook his head, "No, just vanquishing trolls."

Mr. Dyer stood straight up and sniffed the air, "Yes, that was a troll all right. They smell almost as bad as ghouls. Now Brian, there's a big difference between looking out for trouble and just looking for trouble."

"I know, I should have told you first. But this thing's been here for years, in my territory. It's my responsibility. I had to know I could do it. I'm sorry for all the trouble."

Mr. Dyer nodded, "Its okay, but please remember, you need training. This is your territory, yes, but bookworms can work together too. You're my charge, my responsibility. Work with me on this. I was too late to help you this time..."

Brian raised his hands placatingly, nodding in agreement.

"Point well taken. I won't be so foolish in the future."

"Good," Brian's mentor uttered, "Well, I was getting ready for church. Mrs. Dyer was making tea."

He grimaced, then waved his hand in the air, stirring up just enough firmament. Like stepping through a doorway, he climbed into it, into the ABZU.

"Unfortunately for you, this method of transportation only takes you to where you first opened the door. For me that's home, but you've got to walk. Your door is on the other side of the bridge. See you tomorrow in class."

With that, Brian's mentor and school teacher disappeared. Just as abruptly, the firmament faded. Brian waved one hand in front of himself, noticing small trails of golden dust leaving his own fingers. He could just barely feel the tingling. Trying a new skill was a tempting thought, but he decided that he'd had enough adventure for one day. He wanted to go home, not just to the other end of the bridge. After all, it was a great morning for a brisk walk.

Afterward

Chadwick put his paintbrush down and rubbed his eyes. Usually the sensation of working with his hands, especially painting on a big canvas, helped him, made things better. They never went away, the voices. But he could stifle them, press them down in his mind, appease them. This new voice, however, was not going to be ignored.

About the Author

Jon Coley lives in Georgia with his wife, daughters, an orange cat, and an eccentric husky.

Made in the USA
Coppell, TX
10 January 2023